ABOUT THE BANK STREET READY-TO-READ SERIES

More than seventy-five years of educational research, innovative teaching, and quality publishing have earned The Bank Street College of Education its reputation as America's most trusted name in early childhood education.

Because no two children are exactly alike in their development, the Bank Street Ready-to-Read series is written on three levels to accommodate the individual stages of reading readiness of children ages three through eight.

○ *Level 1:* **GETTING READY TO READ (Pre-K–Grade 1)**
Level 1 books are perfect for reading aloud with children who are getting ready to read or just starting to read words or phrases. These books feature large type, repetition, and simple sentences.

● *Level 2:* **READING TOGETHER (Grades 1–3)**
These books have slightly smaller type and longer sentences. They are ideal for children beginning to read by themselves who may need help.

○ *Level 3:* **I CAN READ IT MYSELF (Grades 2–3)**
These stories are just right for children who can read independently. They offer more complex and challenging stories and sentences.

All three levels of the Bank Street Ready-to-Read books make it easy to select the books most appropriate for your child's development and enable him or her to grow with the series step by step. The levels purposely overlap to reinforce skills and further encourage reading.

We feel that making reading fun is the single most important thing anyone can do to help children become good readers. We hope you will become part of Bank Street's long tradition of learning through sharing.

The Bank Street College of Education

To May Garelick
— B.B.

To my daughter, Ana, and son, Pablo
— J.G.

For a free color catalog describing Gareth Stevens' list of high-quality books and multimedia programs, call 1-800-542-2595 (USA) or 1-800-461-9120 (Canada). Gareth Stevens Publishing's Fax: (414) 225-0377.

Library of Congress Cataloging-in-Publication Data

Brenner, Barbara.
    Moon boy / by Barbara Brenner; illustrated by Jesús Gabán.
      p. cm. -- (Bank Street ready-to-read)
    Summary: A moonbeam comes to life one night and visits a young boy.
    ISBN 0-8368-1778-8 (lib. bdg.)
    [1. Moon--Fiction. 2. Night--Fiction.] I. Gabán, Jesús, ill. II. Title.
  III. Series.
  PZ7.B7518Mo   1999
  [E]--dc21   98-38474

This edition first published in 1999 by
Gareth Stevens Publishing
1555 North RiverCenter Drive, Suite 201
Milwaukee, Wisconsin 53212 USA

Printed in Mexico

1 2 3 4 5 6 7 8 9 03 02 01 00 99

Bank Street Ready-to-Read™

Moon Boy

by Barbara Brenner
Illustrated by J. Gabán

A Byron Preiss Book

Gareth Stevens Publishing
MILWAUKEE

It was late.
I couldn't sleep.

I stood at my window
and looked out into the dark.
The stars were far away.

The moon was a gold balloon.

I saw a small streak of light fall.
"Shooting star!"
I said to myself.

Just then a shiny dot
landed on my windowsill.

It grew until it was
a golden stream that turned
into a glowing ball of light.

I watched. The ball became
a body and a face.
It was a boy. Small.
Dressed all in white.

"Who are you?" I asked.
"Moon Boy," he said.
"From where?" I asked.
He said, "From there,"
and pointed to the sky.

The moon was a gold balloon.

Now the moon boy stood
in my hand.
Like a little lamp.
Like a night-light
in the shape of a boy.

We talked,
Moon Boy and I.
We played.
He sailed my Noah's Ark
and hid in my house of blocks.

He flew up to my toy shelf
and sat there, singing.
This is the song he sang:

When the moon is a gold balloon,
moon children come out to play.
They ride the clouds
in golden crowds
along the Milky Way.

But soon the moon
began to fade.
Moon Boy said, "It's time."
"Time for what?" I asked.
"Time to go."

"No! Don't go," I said.
But he flew to the sill
as if to leave me.

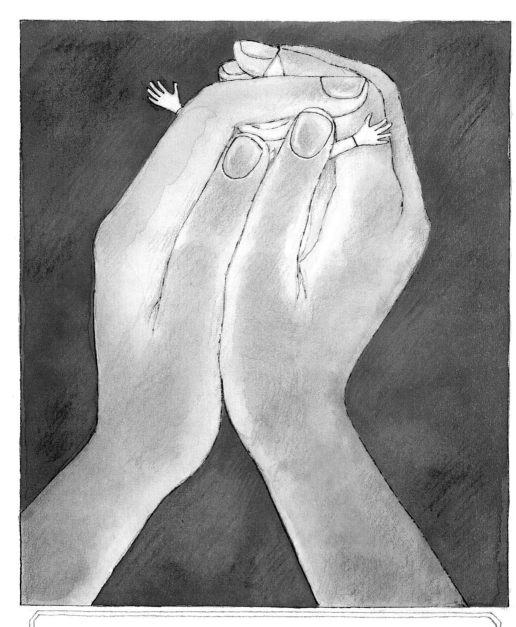

I grabbed him
and held him in my hands.
I spied my toy box,
dropped him in,
and closed the lid tight!

I had him then.
A real moon boy.
To keep like a toy.

But wait . . .
The stars were going out.
The sky turned black.
There was no light.

No moon. No gold balloon.

"What is it?" I cried.
I was afraid.
And then I heard Moon Boy
calling to me from the dark.

"The lights are out
because I am in here.
The moon children
and the stars are sad.

They miss me.
They need me."

I knew then
I would have
to let him go.
A moonbeam is not a toy.
You can't hold it
or lock it in a box.
You need to let it go.

I opened the box
and set the moon boy free.
Once again,

the moon was a gold balloon.

By and by the stars faded.
The moon went in.
I closed my eyes and fell asleep.

In the morning
the sun came out,
and I woke up.
As always.

Barbara Brenner is the author of more than thirty-five books for children, including *Wagon Wheels,* an ALA Notable Book. She writes frequently on subjects related to parenting and is co-author of *Choosing Books for Kids* and *Raising a Confident Child* in addition to being a Senior Editor for the Bank Street College Media Group. Ms. Brenner and her husband, illustrator Fred Brenner, have two sons. They live by a lake in Lords Valley, Pennsylvania.

Jesús Gabán was born in a village near Madrid. He has been illustrating children's books since 1981 and was awarded the Spanish National Prize for Children's Book Illustration in 1984 and 1988. Mr. Gabán's books have been published in Spain, France, Germany, Japan, and the United Kingdom. This is his first book for an American audience.